GEMSTONE DRAGONS

OPAL'S TIME TO SHINE

The Gemstone Dragons series

GEMSTONE DRAGONS

OPAL'S TIME TO SHINE

SAMANTHA M. CLARK

ILLUSTRATED BY
JANELLE ANDERSON

BLOOMSBURY
CHILDREN'S BOOKS
NEW YORK   LONDON   OXFORD   NEW DELHI   SYDNEY

BLOOMSBURY CHILDREN'S BOOKS
Bloomsbury Publishing Inc., part of Bloomsbury Publishing Plc
1385 Broadway, New York, NY 10018

BLOOMSBURY, BLOOMSBURY CHILDREN'S BOOKS, and the Diana logo
are trademarks of Bloomsbury Publishing Plc

First published in the United States of America in August 2022
by Bloomsbury Children's Books

Text copyright © 2022 by Samantha M. Clark
Illustrations copyright © 2021 by Janelle Anderson

Bloomsbury books may be purchased for business or promotional use. For information
on bulk purchases please contact Macmillan Corporate and Premium Sales Department at
specialmarkets@macmillan.com

Library of Congress Cataloging-in-Publication Data
Names: Clark, Samantha M., author. | Anderson, Janelle O., illustrator.
Title: Opal's time to shine / Samantha M. Clark ; illustrated by Janelle O. Anderson.
Description: New York : Bloomsbury Children's Books, [2022] |
Series: Gemstone dragons ; 1 | Audience: Grades 2–3
Summary: The Gemstone Dragons all have unique magical powers, so when Opal,
who has the power of invisibility and does not like being the center of attention,
faces a crisis threatening the Friendship Festival, she must step up to save the day.
Identifiers: LCCN 2021048225 (print) | LCCN 2021048226 (e-book) |
ISBN 978-1-5476-0888-1 (paperback) • ISBN 978-1-5476-0890-4 (e-book)
Subjects: CYAC: Fantasy. | Magic—Fiction. | Dragons—Fiction. | Self confidence—Fiction. |
Friendship—Fiction. | LCGFT: Fantasy fiction.
Classification: LCC PZ7.1.C579 Op 2022 (print) | LCC PZ7.1.C579 (e-book) |
DDC [Fic]—dc23
LC record available at https://lccn.loc.gov/2021048225
LC ebook record available at https://lccn.loc.gov/2021048226

Book design by Jeanette Levy
Typeset by Westchester Publishing Services
Printed in the U.S.A.
6 8 10 9 7 5

To find out more about our authors and books visit www.bloomsbury.com
and sign up for our newsletters.

For Christine,

the biggest dragon fan I know

Gemstone Dragons

OPAL'S TIME TO SHINE

chapter one

A WATERY PROBLEM

Opal stretched up onto her toes, holding two picture frames as high on the cave wall as she could.

"Here?" She peered over her shoulder at her friend, but Aquamarine was frowning.

"It's difficult to see what it'll look like with you standing there." Aquamarine twitched his wings.

"That's no problem." Opal concentrated

on the opal gemstone on her chest and felt its power flow through her body. Her rainbow scales rippled as she turned invisible. Now the picture frames were all that could be seen hanging from the cave wall. "What do you think now?"

Aquamarine scrunched up his nose. "I don't know if I want them both there."

"You'd better hurry up and decide or we'll be late for dinner," Opal said.

Aquamarine waved his paw. "We've got plenty of time. I promise we won't be late."

"I hope not. Tonight Sapphire's going to announce which Gemstone Dragon will give the Friendship Festival speech. I wonder who it'll be." Opal gasped. "Maybe it'll be you, Aquamarine!"

"Me? Nah. I gave it a while ago." He

walked to the other side of his cave to view his decorations from a different angle. "I think it should be you. You've never given the Friendship Festival speech. You'd be great!"

Opal toppled off her toes. "Me? You're funny." She laughed, then stretched to hold the frames up again. "I hope it's Topaz. I loved the speech she gave last year. It was so inspiring!"

"All she did was talk about the sun, and how we need to be the light. We don't need light. We need brilliance!" Aquamarine raised his arms as if to demonstrate how brilliant his cave would be . . . if only he could decide where to put the pictures. He dropped his arms again. "Try making one disappear."

Opal chuckled, then concentrated on her opal gemstone. The picture frame in her left paw disappeared. "How's this?"

Aquamarine flopped down on his bed. "I don't know. Something's not right but I can't put my claw on it. Give me the disappeared frame. Maybe it'll look better with each picture on a different side."

Opal handed the frame to him, but it went right through his outstretched paw. "Sorry, I keep forgetting that when I make something invisible it can go through things. Hold on," she said.

Opal made herself and the frame visible again, then handed it over. Aquamarine placed it against the wall over his bedrock, but shook his head. "That's not it."

Opal glanced at the frame she still had

in her paw. She had never been good at making decisions either. That's why she decorated her bedcave with flowers and changed them every week.

"I don't know, Aquamarine," she said, placing the frame on his rock desk. "But you need to decide quickly. Everyone from Gemstone Valley is going to be at dinner for the announcement, and Shimmering Hall will be packed! I want to get a good seat."

Aquamarine didn't seem concerned. He scanned the walls of his bedcave, then cried, "I know! It's not the pictures that are in the wrong place. It's the stream!" He pointed at the thin stream of water that ran down the wall of his bedcave and across the floor.

"But you love the stream," Opal said. "Water is your gemstone power. Isn't that why you requested this cave in the first place?"

Aquamarine laughed big and loud. "Of course I love the stream. It's my favorite part, but it'll look better running the other way."

The aquamarine gem on his chest glowed as he called on its power. With his light blue scales rippling, Aquamarine strode across the cave, and the stream moved with him.

Opal's bright eyes widened. She loved watching the other Gemstone Dragons use their powers. The dragons and their gemstones joined together to produce something wonderful. Opal had never thought her power of invisibility was particularly special or useful, unless you needed some dragon to hold up a decoration without getting in the way. But Aquamarine could control water, and Opal thought that was an amazing and helpful gift.

Even if it was being used to decorate a bedcave.

Once Aquamarine had the stream flowing down the opposite wall and diagonally across the floor, he grinned.

"There! Now the stream isn't hidden by my bedrock. And I can even lie down in it if I want to." He spread out on the floor, letting the water drip off the wall and onto his snout.

Opal laughed. "I don't think you'll be

taking baths in this tiny stream any time soon, but the placement is nice."

"Yes, I like it here, but you're right." Aquamarine clambered back up, and his gemstone glowed again. "It should be bigger!"

Commotion in the hallway outside the entrance to Aquamarine's bedcave caught

Opal's attention. The other Gemstone Dragons rushed past, chatting excitedly. They were all heading to Shimmering Hall.

Opal glanced back at her friend, who had made the stream twice as big already.

"Let's finish up later, Aquamarine. We're going to miss the announcement," she said. "Oh, I can't wait for the Friendship Festival. I love how everyone in Gemstone Valley spends the whole week working together to gather food and crystals to share. And we have the best celebrations every night. It's my favorite time of the year. Come on!"

Opal grabbed the tip of Aquamarine's wing and dragged him out. Then the two friends hurried with the others to Shimmering Hall.

chapter two

A BIG ANNOUNCEMENT

Shimmering Hall was packed when Opal and Aquamarine walked through the entrance. Almost every seat at the rock tables was taken.

"Do you think we missed the announcement?" Opal whispered.

"Nah. If we had, everyone would be celebrating," Aquamarine said. "Sapphire's probably waiting until after dinner, like last time. I hope so. I could eat a whole clay pit! Come on, let's find some seats."

As Aquamarine led the way through the rock tables, Opal peered through the crowd to see Sapphire. The hall was filled with all the Gemstone Dragons, as well as all the creatures the dragons protected in Gemstone Valley. The unicorns and goblins and gnomes were there. Even the fairies had come to hear who'd be giving the Friendship Festival speech.

Finally, Opal caught a glimpse of Sapphire and smiled. Opal thought Sapphire was the most majestic of all the Gemstone Dragons. The sapphire on her chest was twice the size of the other dragons' gems, and her scales were a deep blue, like the color of the deepest ocean.

Now her scales shined brightly in the multicolored light that filtered through the gem picture behind her.

The wall at the end of Shimmering Hall held more gems than any other part of Sparkle Cave, where all the Gemstone Dragons lived inside Mineral Mountain. There were diamonds, emeralds, and rubies, amber, aquamarines, and even opals. The gems spread across the wall in the shape of a giant Gemstone Dragon. Every time a new Gemstone Dragon egg hatched, that dragon's gem was magically added to the picture, instantly connecting the new dragon with all the others. And when the sun shone through all the gems, it looked like the Gemstone Dragon was blazing with brilliant colors that touched every part of the hall. It amazed Opal every time she saw it.

"Here are two seats together," Aquamarine said, stopping at a rock table where a unicorn and a goblin were chatting. Aquamarine sniffed the air. "Mmmmm. Smells like we're having sulfur muffins with gypsum stew for dinner. Delicious!"

When Topaz and Ruby brought in the trays of food a second later, Opal marveled that Aquamarine had been right. Huge platters of sulfur muffins, spiced with boron and rosemary, were piled in front of them. Plus, there were giant bowls of gypsum and clay stew with basil and lemon, and blueberry carrot pie with slices of yummy zinc on top for dessert.

Opal's tummy rumbled. She was

hungrier than she had thought. She dug into the feast while keeping an eye on Sapphire, who would announce the exciting news.

Before long, Sapphire stood up and let out a gentle roar to get everyone's attention. Sapphire was the oldest and wisest of all the Gemstone Dragons, and when she spoke, everyone listened. All across Shimmering Hall, the talking stopped.

Anticipation bubbled up inside Opal.

"Gemstone Dragons—and all of our friends in Gemstone Valley," Sapphire began, "it's almost time for our Friendship Festival, and what a fantastic festival it's going to be!"

The crowd whooped and applauded.

Opal clapped her paws as hard as she could.

"Emerald has been hard at work on the crystal fields and clay gardens," Sapphire continued. "And our friends in Gemstone Valley have an impressive crop of fruits, vegetables, and herbs. I want to thank them for all they have done. And to everyone who helps cultivate our incredible food, thank you."

More applause billowed across Shimmering Hall. Opal glanced at all the happy faces. This was wonderful.

"Of course, we also want to give a hearty thank you to Topaz, Ruby, and the gnomes who cooked up tonight's delicious feast. I'm sure you enjoyed it as much as I did."

Sapphire rubbed her tummy to show her satisfaction.

"Woo-hoo, Topaz!" shouted one of the unicorns.

"Go, Ruby, Ruby, Ruby!" cried a group of fairies at once.

Opal beamed at the gnomes, who nodded their heads in appreciation.

Sapphire cleared her throat. "And now it's time to start our preparations for the Friendship Festival. With all the goodies we'll be collecting and sharing, the weeklong festival looks like it could be our biggest one yet! And Jade and I have been coming up with fun celebrations to end every single day. I know you'll love them."

She paused and peered around the crowd. A thrill ran through Opal's scales.

This was it! Sapphire was going to announce who would give the Friendship Festival closing speech.

"As you know, the biggest celebrations of the festival are the closing ceremonies," Sapphire said, her regal voice echoing throughout Shimmering Hall. "We listen to the wisdom of one of our most beloved Gemstone Dragons, then enjoy a light-and-wind show by Topaz and Diamond. Plus, lots of good food, of course!"

Sapphire smiled at the crowd, and Topaz and Diamond waved from the front table.

"And now, the moment you've all been waiting for," Sapphire said, her golden eyes twinkling.

Opal and Aquamarine shared an excited grin, then turned back to Sapphire.

"The Gemstone Dragon I've chosen to give our Friendship Festival speech is . . ." Sapphire gazed around at all of the eager faces.

Opal leaned forward, ready to clap loudly for the chosen dragon.

Shimmering Hall fell silent as the crowd waited for Sapphire to speak. Finally, she took in a deep breath and shouted, "OPAL!"

The cave erupted in cheers. Aquamarine clapped Opal on the back. "I knew it! I knew it!" He enveloped Opal in a huge hug. "I'm so proud of you!"

Everyone in the hall was applauding and hollering. Everyone, that is, except Opal. She stared at all those eyes staring back at her. She heard the echo of her name.

And she turned herself invisible.

chapter three

A BIG NO-CAN-DO

Opal was sitting on the rocks at the top of Mineral Mountain Falls when Aquamarine found her.

"You know, trying to find a Gemstone Dragon who has the power to disappear is really hard." He plopped down next to her. "Why'd you leave? Everyone's looking for you to tell you congratulations. They're so excited to hear your speech. I am too."

Opal shook her head. "I can't give the speech."

"Why not?"

"Because . . ." Opal gazed down at the frothy water. "Sapphire made a mistake. She couldn't have meant me. I haven't done anything to deserve it."

"Opal, you're just as deserving as the other dragons. Everyone loves you. Whenever anyone feels bad, you make them feel better—like how you're patient with me and my decorating." Aquamarine grinned. "At the festival, we'll all be celebrating you, Opal."

Aquamarine's gemstone glowed, and streams of water left the falls and rose into the air, forming a big *OPAL* in the sky.

Opal made herself invisible.

"Opal!" Aquamarine scrambled up and glanced around, as if he was worried she'd flown off. "Come back."

Opal sighed and made herself visible again.

"What's wrong?" Aquamarine asked. "You love watching other Gemstone Dragons give those speeches."

"That's just it," Opal said. "I'll have to stand in front of all the Gemstone Dragons and everyone who lives in Gemstone Valley. All the unicorns and gnomes and fairies will be looking at me. And all the other dragons! I'll mess it up. I'll make a complete fool out of myself. I won't be able to speak."

"You talk to me all the time," Aquamarine said. "You'll do great. It's time for you to show off all your awesomeness. I'll even help you."

Opal glanced at her friend. "You will?"

"Sure. You just need a good joke to open with. Hmmm." Aquamarine scrunched up his snout, thinking. "Got it! Why are dragons the best storytellers?"

Opal shrugged.

"Because we've got tails! Get it?" Aquamarine laughed, rolling onto his back as he swished his own tail. "Like, 'tales'?"

Opal smiled. She liked that her friend was trying to make her feel better, but she still didn't think she could do the speech. "Thank you for helping me, Aquamarine. You're the best friend any Gemstone Dragon could ever want. I'm glad you believe in me."

Even though she wasn't sure she believed in herself.

Opal gazed out at Gemstone Valley and sighed. "I'm going to go for a quick fly before bedtime. I'll see you tomorrow, okay?"

"Okay, Opal." Aquamarine gave his friend a hug. "And I know one thing for sure: I will be in the front row when you give your speech at the Friendship Festival." He smiled, then jumped into the frothing water and surfed the falls down to the entrance of Sparkle Cave at the bottom of Mineral Mountain.

Opal opened her wings and pushed off into the sky. The sun was starting to set, and below her, Gemstone Valley was aglow in golden light.

She loved swooping through the valley at this time of the day. Wind surged against her scales as she flew past gnome huts, around goblin hills, and over unicorn stables.

Some unicorns were installing a new jumping ring, and Opal stopped to watch. Bramble was tugging a rope in his teeth to pull the ring upward. As he stepped back and back, the ring rose higher and higher. It was very tall, much taller than the old one. Opal smiled. With this new ring, the unicorns' next jumping contest was sure to be even more amazing. She was already looking forward to it.

And she wasn't the only one. Some of the unifoals were frolicking under the ring, excited to see it up. Opal chuckled to herself then started to glide away, but a shout brought her attention back to the ring.

Bramble had tripped. His hooves stumbled, and the ring started to topple.

It was going to fall right on top of the frolicking unifoals!

Quickly, Opal made herself invisible and dove down. Sweeping under the ring, she caught it before it hit the unifoals. Other unicorns had come to Bramble's rescue, so three unicorns now pulled the rope. Opal lifted the ring too, gently holding it in place while the unicorns secured it.

As the unicorns congratulated each other, Opal took off into the sky again, smiling to herself. One thing she did like about her gemstone power was that she could help others without them knowing.

Then nobody could make a big deal out of it. Opal got flustered when lots of other creatures were around, especially when they all wanted to talk to her. She couldn't bear the thought of standing in front of all of Gemstone Valley to give the Friendship Festival speech. She'd be terrible.

Every speech she'd heard had been amazing. Aquamarine had talked about how Gemstone Dragon power flowed through each of the dragons and into the valley just like the water in the falls. Emerald had talked about how wonderfully all the citizens lived together like an ecosystem. And last year, Topaz had talked about how they were all like light, guiding each other.

Opal got a shiver just thinking about

their speeches. She felt so proud to be friends with all these incredible Gemstone Dragons, but she could never be as inspiring as the others. She was happy being their support from behind the scenes.

That's why she couldn't understand why Sapphire had chosen her. Sapphire was the wisest Gemstone Dragon Opal knew. So why didn't Sapphire know she'd made a bad choice picking Opal?

Approaching Sparkle Cave, Opal pulled her wings in tight and glided through her bedcave window.

"Tomorrow I will fix this," she told herself as she brushed her teeth. "I'll just tell Sapphire she was wrong and has to pick someone else."

But as Opal climbed into her bedrock,

her tummy squirmed. Telling Sapphire she'd made a bad choice made Opal almost as nervous as doing the speech. But she didn't see any other way.

chapter four

MISSION IMPOSSIBLE

The next morning, Opal woke up as soon as the first sunbeam sparked through the window of her bedcave. Usually, she liked to snuggle under her covers as she watched the sun stretch over Gemstone Valley. The flowers in her room would wake up with her, reaching out for the sun's warmth. Opal would take her time, soaking up the morning before joining the others in Shimmering Hall for breakfast.

But this morning was different. This morning, Opal had a mission. She had to find Sapphire and make her change her mind about the closing speech of the Friendship Festival.

Opal jumped out of bed, brushed her teeth until they sparkled, and mopped her scales until they shined. She liked to look her best when she was going to do something difficult, and telling Sapphire that she was wrong felt very difficult.

Opal's heart thumped in her chest as she hurried to Shimmering Hall. If she got to breakfast early enough, she hoped she could catch Sapphire before it got busy.

There was no way she could talk about this in front of others.

But when she arrived in Shimmering Hall, no one was inside. She was too early.

"This is good," Opal told herself, glancing at her shaking paws. "I can't talk to Sapphire yet anyway. I don't even know what to say. I'll go for a walk. That'll help me think of something good. Maybe Aquamarine will come too. He did say he'd help."

She dashed to Aquamarine's bedcave, peered around the entrance, then sighed. Aquamarine had tripled the size of the stream flowing through his cavern. He must've been up half the night working on it. Now he was sleeping with a big smile on his face as the water sloshed around him. Opal didn't have the heart to wake him up. She'd have to figure out what to say to Sapphire on her own.

Opal strolled out into the dawn and breathed in the fresh morning air. Gemstone Valley was just starting to wake up, and she could see yawning unicorns and gnomes shuffling out of their homes. Opal made her way into the villages, muttering to herself about what she could say to Sapphire.

"Hi, Sapphire. How are you? It looks like it's going to be a beautiful day today. The birds are singing . . ."

Opal shook her head. "Sapphire's busy. Get to the point." She took a deep breath then tried again. "Hi, Sapphire. I want to tell—"

"Hey, Opal!"

Opal glanced up to see one of the younger unifoals, Canterlope, waving to her. Opal smiled shyly back.

"I can't wait for your speech," Canterlope said.

Opal frowned. She didn't want to be rude and not answer, but her mouth had gone dry. How could Canterlope be looking forward to her speech? She turned down another path and began thinking about what to say to Sapphire again.

"Hello, Sapphire. I am very flattered that you chose me to give the Friendship Festival speech, but . . . I'm going to be too busy that day." Opal shook her tail. "I can't lie, and besides, Sapphire's never going to believe that. Everyone stops what they're doing for the speech."

"Happy morning to you, Opal." Braidenbeard, one of the gnomes she'd seen at the big dinner last night, leaned out of his window and waved at her. "Wonderful news!"

Opal gave him an uneasy smile as her tummy churned. Braidenbeard was happy for her too? She hurried away.

"Sapphire," Opal tried a third time, "you are the wisest dragon in all of Gemstone Valley, and I appreciate your confidence in me, but I . . ."

"Ooooh, Opal!" Three tiny fairies fluttered in front of Opal's face. Opal took a step backward. "We were so thrilled to hear you'd been chosen for the big celebration," they said in unison. "We will make you the biggest daisy chain to wear," said one. "With sweet smelling geraniums," said another. "And bright pink posies," said the third. "It

will be divine," they said together, then gave Opal a high-pitched giggle.

"Oh, uh, thank you," Opal said, stepping backward so fast she tripped over her tail and fell flat on her rump. She quickly concentrated on the power in her gemstone, and with a ripple of her scales she disappeared.

"Where'd she go?" asked the fairies together. "I don't know," they answered each other. "Oh well, let's get breakfast; then we can start on her chain."

They flew away, and Opal turned off her invisibility. She clenched her paws to stop them from shaking.

Her being chosen for the Friendship Festival speech was even worse than she'd thought. Her friends were excited for her, but she just knew that if she actually did give the speech, they'd all be horribly disappointed.

She pushed herself up and strode back toward Sparkle Cave, more nervous than ever. She had to find the perfect words to make Sapphire change her mind, but nothing seemed right. Frustrated, she finally blurted out what she really wanted to say, "Sapphire, you've made a big mistake!"

"Have I?"

Opal's breath caught in her throat. She whirled around to find Sapphire strolling into Sparkle Cave behind her.

"I . . ." Opal couldn't think of any good words to say. She could barely think of any words at all! "I . . ."

Sapphire smiled down at Opal. "A

morning walk is wonderful for getting the old muscles and brain working, don't you think?"

Opal had never really thought about it before. "I . . . suppose so."

"I love to see all our friends in Gemstone Valley as they start their day," Sapphire continued.

Opal gulped. Had Sapphire seen her walking around? Had she heard her mumbling? Had she seen the unicorn and gnome and fairies congratulating her?

"Now," Sapphire said, "you were saying something about a mistake I had made."

Opal gazed at the ground. "Uh, well . . ."

"I'm afraid I've made many, many mistakes in my many, many years,"

Sapphire said. "And I'm sure I'm going to make many more. They can be terribly useful for learning. So what mistake have I made now?"

Opal looked up and saw Sapphire's eyes were twinkling.

Opal wanted to disappear, but then she'd never get out of doing the speech. She swallowed, then said, "It's just, I'm very honored that you've chosen me to speak at the Friendship Festival, but, you see, I can't do it."

"Oh? Why not?"

"I . . . I'm just not good at that sort of thing. And besides, I'm not special like the other Gemstone Dragons." Opal beamed, thinking of the other dragons. "Emerald is so fantastic with plants. Amber can fix anything. And Aquamarine tells the best jokes."

Sapphire nodded with each of Opal's words. "True. True. They are all quite wonderful."

A burst of hope sparked inside Opal. Sapphire agreed!

"I chose you for a reason, Opal," Sapphire said, and Opal held her breath. "But if you feel strongly that I've made a mistake, I will give you an opportunity to prove it. If you can find another dragon that all the other Gemstone Dragons would prefer to hear from at the Friendship Festival, I will ask them to speak instead. But we are on a deadline. I'll need their name by dinner tonight."

Opal let out her breath. "No problem,

Sapphire. Thank you. You won't be disappointed. I'll find the best Gemstone Dragon for the speech. I promise!"

Sapphire smiled warmly. "I know you will. Now, if you'll excuse me, I believe I smell eggplant and silicon at breakfast. My favorite."

Opal watched Sapphire walk into Shimmering Hall, but she didn't follow. She was far too excited. She had done it! She had talked to Sapphire and gotten what she wanted—at least, she would get it soon. All she had to do was find out who the other Gemstone Dragons thought should give the speech. Then Sapphire would ask them. That would be the easy part.

She hoped.

chapter five

A PLAN IN ACTION

Opal wanted to get to work on Sapphire's task immediately, but the idea of talking to all the dragons about something this important made her insides squirm. She needed Aquamarine's help. He could talk to any dragon. Everyone loved him. She hoped he was awake by now.

Hurrying through the Sparkle Cave

passageways toward Aquamarine's bed-cave, Opal turned a corner and . . .

CRASH!

Twigs and sticks flew in every direction, clattering to the ground and onto Opal's scales.

"Oh no!" Ruby rushed out of her bedcave. "I'm so sorry, Opal."

"I'm okay, but what are you doing with all these twigs?" Opal asked, brushing a twig off her snout.

"I'm setting up a big bonfire in my bedcave so I can practice controlling my fire. This is the first batch of wood I've collected. See?" Ruby pointed at the pile of twigs she was building next to her bedrock. She looked very proud of herself.

"That sounds like fun," Opal said. "It's

great that you're practicing, but, um, don't you think it'd be safer to practice your fire outside? You'd have a lot more space."

Ruby glanced from her pile of twigs to the open fields outside her window. "That's a good idea! Can you help me carry them out?"

"Sure." Opal grabbed a heap of twigs and sticks and followed Ruby through the passageway toward the Sparkle Cave entrance. "Hey, Ruby, I want to ask you something."

"What is it?"

"Who do you think would be the best dragon to give the Friendship Festival speech?"

"Oh, I forgot to tell you congratulations!" Ruby dropped the sticks she was carrying and ran to Opal, hugging her around her middle as the twigs in Opal's arms went flying. "I can't wait to hear your speech."

"No, I don't mean me." Opal picked up the twigs again. "If you could hear a speech

from any of the Gemstone Dragons, who would you choose?"

Ruby looked surprised, but she thought about it. Finally, she shrugged. "I'd like to hear you."

"No," Opal said, "think of Amber. She knows about everything. Or Aquamarine. He's always so funny. Or maybe Diamond."

Ruby stopped retrieving sticks and scrunched up her snout. "Diamond is so pushy sometimes. He never lets me eat what I want to." She glanced around. "Don't tell him I said that. He'll put more nitrogen in my oatmeal. He keeps saying it'll make my fire hotter, but it's so bitter. No, I want you to give the speech, Opal. You're going to be great."

Opal sighed. This wasn't going as well as she'd hoped. Maybe she hadn't explained it properly. She really needed Aquamarine's help. He was so much better at talking to others.

After she'd finished helping Ruby build her bonfire outside, Opal made her way back into Sparkle Cave to find Aquamarine but was stopped in the entrance by Topaz and Diamond.

"Hi, Opal," Diamond said. "We were just talking about you."

"You were?" Opal's claw dug into the cave floor. What could they have been saying about her?

"We're planning the light-and-wind show that will follow your speech," Diamond said. "Have you decided what you'll talk about yet? We can do a show that will match."

Opal's paws felt sweaty. She wanted to disappear immediately. But then she wouldn't be able to accomplish the mission Sapphire had given her. She took a deep breath.

"Actually, I've been wanting to talk to you two as well. I'm interviewing every Gemstone Dragon to see who they'd most like to give the speech. Don't you think it would be amazing to have Emerald tell us how he grows the crystal plants? Or maybe Garnet could tell us what it's like to fly as fast as the wind. What do you think?"

Diamond and Topaz glanced at each other, then back at Opal.

"No way, Opal," said Topaz. "I've been

hoping you'd do the Friendship Festival speech for ages. I can't wait to hear what you say."

Opal frowned. "But . . ."

Diamond clapped his paw on Opal's shoulder. "Let us know when you've got a theme for your speech. We'll work up a brilliant show for after."

Then Diamond and Topaz continued on outside, leaving Opal as confused and worried as she'd ever been. Had they not understood her question? Why was no one choosing another dragon? She had to find Aquamarine. He'd make it clear to everyone.

It was later in the morning, and Opal felt sure Aquamarine was awake by now.

She hurried into Shimmering Hall and finally spotted him piling magma cakes onto a large plate. Opal's stomach rumbled.

"There you are," she said when she caught up to him. She grabbed a magma cake and took a big bite. *Mmm.* These were her favorite. She loved the way the warm magma inside the cake oozed onto her tongue. "I eed or elp!"

Aquamarine laughed. "Slow down. I can't understand a word you're saying."

Opal swallowed the rest of her cake, licking all the magma off her lips before she continued. "I need your help, Aquamarine. I—"

"THEY'RE DYING! THEY'RE ALL

DYING!" Ruby ran into Shimmering Hall, waving her arms frantically over her head. Every dragon dropped their food and turned toward her. Ruby stopped in the middle of the Hall, tears brimming her eyes. "The Friendship Festival is RUINED!"

chapter six

FIELDS OF BROWN

Opal stared at Ruby, then turned to Aquamarine. His eyes were as large as the sun.

Amber strode over to Ruby. "What are
you talking about, Ruby? The Friendship
Festival isn't ruined. Who's dying?"

Ruby shook her head. "Not who. What!
All the crystal plants are brown and brittle.
They're dying!"

Emerald stood up then, his green scales

gleaming in the sunlight streaming through the Gemstone Dragon wall. "What do you mean the crystal plants are brown? I checked them yesterday afternoon, and they were growing beautifully."

Ruby sniffed. "I was just collecting twigs in the forest on the side of Mineral Mountain. I'm building a bonfire outside so I can practice my fire. It's getting really big and—"

"Ruby!" Amber nudged the young red dragon. "The crystal plants."

"Oh, yes!" Ruby turned to Emerald. "The fields looked strange through the trees, so I went to investigate and . . . and . . ." Ruby burst into tears. "The plants are all dying."

Emerald frowned. "You must be mistaken, Ruby. I've been watching the plants carefully every day. These are our best ones yet."

Amber tapped a claw on her snout. "Maybe we should have a look, Emerald. I'm sure everything is fine, but if there is a problem, we can fix it quickly." Her light orange scales shined as she lifted her wings.

Emerald nodded. "Good idea. Let's go."

Emerald and Amber rose into the air. They flew over the heads of the other dragons and out of Shimmering Hall.

"I'm coming too," Ruby said, then turned to Opal. "I'm sorry the Friendship Festival is ruined. Now you won't be able to give your speech."

Ruby flew off, leaving Opal with a stomach that was doing somersaults. She didn't want the Friendship Festival to be ruined. That would be horrible.

But she couldn't deny that a part of her was relieved at the thought of not having to do the speech.

Still, if it meant there would be no festival at all, she'd much rather have the festival. Everyone in Gemstone Valley loved working together during the festival to gather food to share. It didn't matter whether they were dragons, unicorns, gnomes, or one of the other magical creatures. They all worked side by side during the day and celebrated their friendship every night. They couldn't miss out on it.

"Come on," Aquamarine said. "Let's go see what's going on."

"Yes, let's." Opal nodded, and they

followed the others out of Sparkle Cave
and up Mineral Mountain.

When they got to the crystal plant fields,
Opal felt as though a rock had lodged itself
inside her chest. She could immediately
see that Ruby was right. Something was
terribly wrong.

The fields were one of Opal's favorite
places to fly over. There were rows and
rows of glittery green plants with different-
colored crystals hanging off them. It was
like a rainbow growing right on the side of
their mountain.

But now the green
stalks were brown, and
the usually bright
crystals were dull and
cracking.

"I don't know what happened," Emerald said, as Opal and Aquamarine landed. "They were all fine yesterday."

"Ruby was right," Amber said, pulling a broken crystal off a stem. "This really is a disaster."

"The Friendship Festival is ruined, isn't it?" Ruby said, gazing at the fields gloomily.

"Oh Ruby, it's much worse than that," Amber said. "These crystals keep our gemstones strong. If we don't have enough to eat, all our gemstone powers will be gone."

chapter seven

A MYSTERY

Word got around Shimmering Hall quickly, and soon more and more dragons joined them at the crystal plant fields. Opal could hear them gasp and cry out when they saw what had happened to the crystals.

"What are we going to do?" asked Ruby. "I'm just starting to learn how to use my gemstone power. I don't want to lose it."

"Me neither," said Topaz, hugging Ruby.

"We can't have the Friendship Festival now," said Diamond, after he'd inspected the plants. "There's nothing to celebrate."

"How could this happen?" Emerald slumped on the ground.

"Your power makes things grow, Emerald," Amber said. "Can't you help them?"

"I can try." The gemstone in Emerald's chest glowed as he spread out his paws over the nearest crystal plants. His green scales rippled with the power running through them. Beneath his paws, the plants' brown stalks began to brighten and the cracks in its crystals closed.

"It's working!" shouted Ruby, jumping up and down.

But it only lasted for a few seconds. Then the plant drooped closer to the ground, and its crystals dropped onto the earth, shattering into dust.

Emerald cried out. "I don't understand."

"Are you losing your power already?" Topaz's eyes grew wide.

Emerald shrugged. "I feel fine. But the plants aren't responding."

"Where's Sapphire? She'll know what to do," Amber said, glancing around the crowd of dragons.

"I think she's making festival preparations with the gnomes," said Diamond. "But she's not going to be able to fix this. No dragon can!"

The dragons all started talking at once, each more anxious than the next.

Aquamarine looked at Opal. "This is terrible, Opal. I'm sorry you won't get to do your speech."

Opal shook her head. Her speech was the last thing on her mind right now. If the crystal plants couldn't be saved, the Gemstone Dragons would lose their powers, and that would be the worst thing that could ever happen. Aquamarine wouldn't be able to make any more water sculptures. Topaz and Diamond wouldn't be able to do their light-and-wind shows. The dragons wouldn't be able to use their powers to help each other and everyone else in Gemstone Valley.

"This is horrible," Topaz said.

"It's a disaster," Ruby said.

"What if I can never get the plants to grow again?" Emerald said, touching a stalk lovingly.

"It'll be okay," Opal said quietly. But none of the dragons was listening. They were too busy talking about every bad thing that could happen next.

Opal couldn't let them give up. She didn't want them to be worried and scared. She cleared her throat. "Dragons," she said louder, "it'll be okay. We've worked through problems before and we'll get through this one too. You'll see. Amber's right. Sapphire will know what to do."

Amber stood straighter. "Yes, we have to get her here."

Opal turned to Garnet, who was

bouncing on his toes next to Diamond. "Garnet, could you use your gemstone power to fly to Sapphire quickly?"

Garnet stopped bouncing. "I'm on it!" His gemstone began to glow; then, as his pink scales rippled, he spread out his wings and took to the air. He sped off toward Gemstone Valley so fast, he was out of sight in the blink of an eye.

"Good thinking, Opal," Amber said, making Opal blush.

"You're the smart one, Amber," Opal said. "You're always finding solutions to problems. Can you figure out why the plants aren't responding to Emerald's power?"

All the dragons watched as Amber examined the crystal plants. She strode around the fields, Emerald following

closely behind. Amber peered at a stem of
one plant, a leaf of another, then a crystal
of another.

"The leaves are wide enough to get the sun's rays," she said. "And the stalks are sturdy. You've done a great job growing them, Emerald."

"Thank you," Emerald mumbled, but he didn't look any happier.

"But . . ." Suddenly Amber bent down and dug her paw into the earth, lifting the soil. It dusted off her claws easily. "This ground is far too dry. There's not enough moisture. That's it!" Amber stood up quickly. "You're not losing your gemstone power, Emerald. You can't grow things if they don't have everything they need to grow. And these plants are thirsty. Very thirsty!"

Opal beamed at Amber. "Well done, Amber! I knew you could figure it out."

Amber smiled, but only slightly. "Thank

you, Opal. But we haven't fixed the problem yet. I have no idea why the soil is so dry. These fields usually have lots of water. I don't know how that could change so quickly, but without water, there's no way these plants will grow."

"We're doomed," cried Ruby, hugging Topaz again.

Worried murmurs rose from the dragons, but Opal stepped forward. "No, we're not. We're the Gemstone Dragons. We're never doomed as long as we don't give up." She gave them all her most encouraging smile. "Aquamarine, you can do wonderful things with water. You can fix the water problem in the soil, can't you?"

Aquamarine grinned as he puffed up his scales. "Thanks, Opal. I can try. Hey, anyone know what letter has the most water in it?"

The other dragons frowned and shook their heads.

"C! Get it? Like the deep blue sea." Aquamarine waved his paw. "Oh, never mind. Let's get these plants something to drink."

He spread out his light blue wings and lifted off. "I can pull some water over here once I know where it went." He flew higher, shouting down at the dragons. "These fields are fed by the same stream that flows into the waterfall," he explained. "The water comes down the side of Mineral Mountain and splits off, spreading rivulets all across here. But I don't see them now.

They must've dried up. It looks like they've just . . ." He flew a little higher. "Oh."

Aquamarine came back down with a thud.

His face was bright red.

"What is it?" Opal asked.

"I . . ." Aquamarine rubbed his paw across his forehead. "Wow, it's . . . hot out here. Is anyone else hot? I'm hot. I . . ."

"What happened to the water?" Amber asked.

The dragons all crowded around Aquamarine, who took a step backward.

"Well . . . see . . . I didn't think it would change anything. I just wanted my bedcave to look nice."

Diamond frowned. "What are you talking about?"

Aquamarine clenched his paws together. "I might've moved the water a bit."

Ruby gasped. "Aquamarine broke the stream!"

chapter eight

A GROWING SOLUTION

"You broke the stream?" Amber cried.

"Not broke," said Aquamarine. "I just borrowed it . . . a little."

The other dragons looked angry.

"How can you borrow a stream?" shouted Diamond.

"What were you thinking?" asked Emerald.

"Everyone!" said Opal. "He didn't do this on purpose. Right, Aquamarine?"

Aquamarine wasn't his usual happy self. He gazed at the ground, not looking at any of his friends. "I'm sorry. I didn't know this would happen. I didn't mean to hurt anything."

Opal smiled. "See? And now that he's figured out the problem, he just has to move the stream back to where it was before. He can do that. I know he can."

Aquamarine peered at the dragons again. "Umm, yeah, well . . ."

Diamond crossed his arms tightly. "What?"

Aquamarine swallowed. "It's just . . . I'm not sure how the stream was before."

"You moved it without looking?" Amber sighed heavily.

"I was in my bedcave," Aquamarine said. "It's not like I've mapped out all the rivers on the mountain."

The dragons started to shuffle and murmur to each other. Opal could tell they were getting anxious.

"Amber," Opal said, "you know what riverbeds look like, don't you?"

Amber nodded slowly. "I can figure it out. I'll fly high up and point the way. Aquamarine, you can move the water where I point."

Aquamarine straightened. "I can do that."

Amber unfurled her light orange wings

and took to the sky. "Yes, I can see where the water needs to go."

"Great!" Aquamarine shouted. He flapped his light blue wings and rose up as the aquamarine gemstone glowed on his chest. "I've got the river. The water's coming!"

All the dragons took to the sky so they could watch. Flying above the crystal fields, Opal beamed with pride as her friends worked.

"Follow that path," Amber said, pointing. "Spread the water out here."

"I see it!" Aquamarine said, and just as he'd made the stream in his bedcave bigger, he pulled on the streams on the side of Mineral Mountain. Water rushed into the dried up rivulets, seeping into the ground. As Opal watched, the dry, dusty soil turned darker with moisture.

"It's working!" Ruby cried. She flew back to the ground, followed by the other dragons.

But Opal had been watching the flow of water closely. In his hurry to fix the problem, Aquamarine had pulled on the stream really hard. Now a wave of water looked like it was going to crush the crystal plants.

"Aquamarine!" she shouted, pointing at the wave.

He nodded and pulled back on the water, but it wasn't enough. "I'm trying to slow it, but it's too strong!"

"Get something to block it," shouted Amber.

Opal glanced around, but the only things in the field were the crystal plants they were trying to save. "There's nothing!"

Then she had an idea. Just as she had made Aquamarine's picture frame disappear, maybe she could make the wave disappear until it broke and lost its strength. She turned to Aquamarine. "Keep moving the water into the streams. I'm going to try something."

With her gemstone glowing, Opal made herself invisible, then flew to the wave. She sucked in a deep breath and hoped her plan would work.

The wave barreled toward the crystal plants, and Opal swooped alongside it. She could see Aquamarine pull on the water, but it wasn't shifting direction fast enough.

The crystal plants were getting closer! Opal dipped her paws into the froth, accessed her gemstone power, and made the wave disappear.

"What happened?" shouted Amber. "Where did the wave go?"

"I don't know." Aquamarine continued moving the smaller streams to where they should have been.

Opal knew exactly what had happened. She was the only one who could see the wave. Just as they had thought, the wave's crest had plowed right into the crystal plants, but because she had made it disappear, it did no damage at all. A few seconds later, the wave broke and the water drained away from Opal's paws. No longer touching her, the water reappeared, but it didn't matter. The wave had lost all its force, and the water trickled into the soil as Opal turned herself visible again.

"Opal stopped the wave!" shouted Aquamarine, pulling the last of the water back into the correct riverbeds.

"And the streams are back!" Amber cried, landing on the ground with the other dragons. "Thank you, Opal. Great job, Aquamarine."

Aquamarine hung his head. "It wasn't that great. If it wasn't for me, we wouldn't have had this problem in the first place."

Opal placed her paw on his shoulder. "We all make mistakes. It's fixing them that counts."

The other dragons nodded.

Opal turned to Emerald. "Did it work?"

Emerald dug his paw into the soil, bringing up a pawful of mud. He grinned. "The soil is much better now." But Topaz frowned. "The crystal plants still don't look good. What if it's too late to save them?"

"Don't worry, Topaz," Opal said. "We're Gemstone Dragons. We can make everything better when we work together. Right, Emerald, Amber?"

The dragons smiled. "That's right. I should be able to get them growing now." Emerald's gemstone glowed again as he worked on the plants. Slowly, the stems straightened and greened and the shine came back to the crystals.

"Some are not improving," Emerald said, sadly. "They got too dry. They need more time."

"We don't have much time before the festival," Amber said. "Aquamarine, try to get the water into the plants."

"Great idea, Amber!" Opal said. "Emerald, you can use your power at the same time."

Aquamarine and Emerald nodded. As Aquamarine's gemstone cast a light blue glow and Emerald's shined a bright green, the last of the crystal plants came back to life. But the dragons didn't stop there. With their scales rippling, Aquamarine and Emerald sent more of their powers into the fields.

The other dragons gasped as all the plants sprang up even taller and thicker, with more crystals sprouting from the stems.

"You did it!" Opal shouted.

All the dragons cheered.

Just then, Garnet flew overhead, with Sapphire following closely behind.

"What took you so long, Garnet?" Diamond asked as Garnet landed. "You're supposed to be fast. Maybe you need more zinc in your diet."

Garnet glared at him. "I'm the fastest dragon here! But Sapphire had already left the gnomes. I had to look everywhere. I finally found her with the fairies."

"Yes, I'm here!" Sapphire touched down, folding her deep blue wings behind her. "What did I miss?"

chapter nine

MISSION COMPLETE

Dinner that night was a big celebration.
The crystal plants had been saved, and
excitement was growing even more for the
Friendship Festival.

Diamond and Topaz cooked up a meal
fit for royalty, with roasted squash
sprinkled with carbon, fried zinc peppers,
carrot and sodium cakes, and soft graphite
bread. For dessert, they had delicious

rosemary-neon ice cream made super cold and creamy thanks to Pearl's icy gemstone power.

Everyone was buzzing about the day's events, and even though Opal sat quietly at her table with Aquamarine, she could hear her name coming from every corner of the hall.

She couldn't imagine what they were all saying and wanted to turn herself invisible.

But hunger got the better of her. She'd been so busy with the mission Sapphire had given her, as well as the problems with the crystal fields, she'd only had one magma cake all day. She thoroughly enjoyed gobbling up all the wonderful food.

As the dragons were tucking into their ice cream, Opal's stomach started rumbling again, this time with nerves. It was time for her to give her report about the Friendship Festival speech to Sapphire. And she was no better off than she had been that morning.

She glanced at the oldest dragon. Sapphire was sitting at the main table, her blue scales looking even deeper in the waning sunlight that was coming through the Gemstone Dragon picture on the wall behind her. Perhaps Opal could convince Sapphire to give her one more day. It was the only hope she had.

"I'll be right back," Opal told Aquamarine as she stood. Her legs were a little shaky, but she took a deep breath as her friend mumbled an "okay" around his ice cream.

Opal made her way to Sapphire's table, then cleared her throat.

"Um, Sapphire?"

"Opal!" Sapphire beamed at her. "It's lovely to see you. Did you try some of the lava sauce on the ice cream? It's scrumptious."

Opal shook her head, and her stomach gave another nervous tumble. "That sounds wonderful. I'll try some right now."

She took a step away, but Sapphire said, "Before you do, how did it go with my little assignment?"

Opal grimaced. She had to do this now. She turned back to Sapphire.

"Not too well," she said, her back claw

digging into the cave floor. "I didn't have time to talk to many of the Gemstone Dragons because everyone was so busy with the crystal fields."

"I'm sure that was quite exciting." Sapphire's eyes twinkled.

"It was," Opal said, smiling. "It was wonderful to see Amber and Aquamarine and Emerald all working together. They are truly amazing dragons."

"From the stories I've been hearing, there are other dragons we need to thank as well," Sapphire said.

"Absolutely." Opal looked over at the dragons enjoying their dinner. "If it weren't for Ruby, we wouldn't have known about the problem. And Diamond kept everyone in check. All the dragons are great."

"They are indeed." Sapphire nodded. "So I take it that you don't have another recommendation for the Friendship Festival speech."

"Not yet, but if you give me one more day, I can ask everyone and get you a big list of names of dragons who'll be perfect." Opal twitched her tail nervously.

"That sounds great! But, oh wait, I've got an even better idea."

Opal's breath caught in her throat. She hoped Sapphire already had some dragon in mind.

"We've got all the Gemstone Dragons gathered here right now," Sapphire said. "Let's ask them!"

Sapphire stood and gave a short roar to get everyone's attention. Once Shimmering

Hall was quiet and all eyes were on her, Sapphire gave a big broad smile.

"Gemstone Dragons, what an exciting day we've had. I want to give a big round of applause and our deepest gratitude to all the dragons who were instrumental in getting our crystal fields healthy again."

The Hall erupted in cheers and whoops.

"Our Friendship Festival and our crystal plants have been saved, and I for one cannot wait for the celebrations," Sapphire continued. The dragons clapped louder.

"As we prepare, Opal here has made the most wonderful suggestion. Just like the way our dragons came together to save the day, perhaps it shouldn't be up to me to choose the giver of our Friendship Festival speech."

The dragons started to murmur among themselves. Opal took a step back, hoping she was in the shadow. As much as she wanted to disappear now, it would look too obvious. Sapphire quieted the dragons again with a raise of her paw.

"So, while we are all here together, I want to give you the opportunity to nominate the dragon you feel has best embodied the Gemstone spirit this year, the dragon you would like to hear from as we celebrate our great festival. After you've nominated the dragons, we'll all vote on who will give the closing speech." Sapphire paused, glancing around the Hall. Then she waved her paws in invitation. "Who wants to give a nomination first? Just shout out the name. Come on."

The dragons muttered to each other again, and Opal's heartbeat raced. Who would they call out?

Emerald was the first one to stand.

"Good!" said Sapphire. "We have our first nomination. Who would you like to nominate, Emerald?"

"I nominate . . ." He paused as he gazed over the other dragons, then smiled. "Opal!"

Opal gasped. Why was he nominating her?

The dragons clapped. Then Amber stood up. "I nominate Opal too!"

Opal gasped again. She couldn't understand what was happening.

"That's two nominations," Sapphire said matter-of-factly. "Anyone else?"

Ruby jumped up, then Topaz. Together they shouted, "We nominate Opal!"

Opal's gemstone glowed slightly as her invisibility pulled on her, but then she stopped. As unbelievable as it was, these dragons really wanted her to give the speech!

But what about the others?

"Wonderful!" Sapphire said. "We have four nominations for Opal. Let's put it to a vote. All who agree that Opal should give the closing Friendship Festival speech, stand up now."

Aquamarine shot up, then Diamond, then Obsidian. One by one, dragon after dragon stood up until every single Gemstone Dragon was on its feet.

Opal's eyes welled with tears. She had been so convinced that no one wanted to hear what she had to say. How could she have been so wrong?

Sapphire beamed at the dragons, then at Opal. She waved Opal over. "My dear Opal, it looks like it's unanimous. Would you do us all the honor of giving the speech at our Friendship Festival?"

Opal tried to speak, but she was so surprised, she couldn't form any words. Instead she nodded big.

All the Gemstone Dragons cheered.

chapter ten

A CELEBRATION FIT FOR A DRAGON

The Friendship Festival was the best ever. Every day, the dragons, unicorns, gnomes, and all the other magical creatures in Gemstone Valley worked together under the bright sun. They gathered crystals, squash, cucumbers, tomatoes, carrots, and more. They emptied the fields of their bounty, readying everything to be used in big feasts.

Each night, after finishing work, the creatures sang songs around bonfires lit by Ruby, played games like I Spy a Unicorn's Eye, and watched the fairies perform air dances.

Finally, it was the last day of the Friendship Festival. The remainder of the crops were stored away tight in the caves deep under Mineral Mountain. Then all the residents of Gemstone Valley gathered together inside Shimmering Hall.

It was time for Opal's speech.

Opal was glad Aquamarine was standing next to her while she waited at the side of the Hall. As the fairies placed their daisy chain around Opal's neck and sang, "Good luck, Opal," all together, Opal's stomach did nervous flips.

"You have nothing to worry about, Opal," Aquamarine said as the fairies flew to their seats. "I wanted to be the first to nominate you, but I knew that if I had, you would've said the other dragons joined in just because of me."

Opal smiled. "You're right. I would've said that."

"Now, if you need a joke to open with, I came up with a good one: How do you know how much a dragon weighs?"

Opal thought but couldn't think of an answer. "I don't know. How do you know how much a dragon weighs?"

"You look at their scales."

Aquamarine giggled. Opal giggled. Soon they were both rolling over laughing.

"I see you're enjoying the speech-giving

already," Sapphire said, striding toward them.

Opal and Aquamarine quickly stood up.

"Sorry, Sapphire," Aquamarine said. "Just giving Opal some pointers. Not that she'll need them. Knock their tails off, Opal." Then he went to take his seat.

Sapphire turned to Opal. "Are you ready?"

Opal nodded, although her paws were still shaking. Sapphire saw this and clamped her steady paws around Opal's. "It's okay to be nervous. That shows that this matters to you. Nothing worth doing is ever easy," she said with a wink.

Opal gave Sapphire a small smile. "I guess so."

Sapphire leaned closer to Opal so that

only she could hear the next words. "Remember, I said I had a reason for choosing you to give this speech. Do you want to know what it is?"

Opal nodded. She really did.

"Whenever I hear about good things happening in Gemstone Valley or Mineral Mountain, there's one name that's mentioned more than any other." Sapphire paused to gaze at Opal. "It's not the first name in the story or the dragon who did the biggest action. Those names come and go depending on what the problem was. But there's one dragon whose name is always in the story. The dragon who's in the background supporting all the others. She encourages them. She calms them. She lets them know that if they just are themselves, they can accomplish anything. She isn't taking the glory, but she's making the biggest difference.

"That name, that dragon, is you, Opal." Sapphire put her paws on both of Opal's shoulders. "You are a very special Gemstone Dragon, Opal. You use your powers, not just of invisibility, but of kindness, to always hold up those around you. And that is powerful indeed."

Sapphire gave Opal a tight hug, so tight Opal had to hold her breath. Finally, the older dragon released Opal and said, "Thank you. Now go and share your gifts with us."

Opal didn't know what to say. She had always tried to stay behind the scenes, to be invisible as she helped others shine. She had never imagined that would make her be seen too.

"Thank you, Sapphire," Opal said, then walked to the front of the Hall.

Every eye was on Opal now. All the residents of Gemstone Valley and all the other dragons were looking at her. But she didn't mind as much anymore. She took a deep breath and began her speech.

"Gemstone Dragons and everyone from Gemstone Valley, I am honored and happy to speak to you today. I'll admit that I didn't think I was the right dragon to give this speech. But now I know that every dragon has something good to give. You don't have to be big like Sapphire, or strong like Obsidian. You don't have to be super smart

like Amber or really fast like Garnet. You don't even have to have a gemstone power. Each and every one of you does amazing things, big and small, to help the creatures around you. Gemstone Valley wouldn't be the same without everyone here. Only together are we at our best."

Gazing at the faces looking at her, Opal told all her favorite stories about times the dragons and other creatures had come together to help each other. "When you do even the smallest thing for someone else, even just give a smile or nice word, we all see you," she said. "We all thank you. We all love you."

When she was finished, the Hall erupted in applause and cheers. Opal beamed brighter than the setting sunrays coming through the Gemstone Dragon wall picture behind her.

Sapphire thanked Opal, then invited everyone to go outside to view Diamond and Topaz's light-and-wind show. As they filed out, dragons, gnomes, and other magical creatures congratulated Opal and told her which stories they loved best.

Aquamarine joined Opal grinning. "I knew you'd be great. You only forgot one story."

"Which one was that?" Opal asked.

"The one where you finish helping me decorate my bedcave. It's still all wrong, Opal. I can't do it without you." Aquamarine winked.

Opal laughed. "I'll help you tomorrow. But first . . ."

"Let's watch!" Aquamarine finished.

They found a good spot on the grass just as the sun was setting. As the last red rays drained away, Topaz's white lights lit up the sky again.

The crowd oohed and aahed as Topaz threw lightbeams into the air and Diamond scattered them with his wind power. The lights streaked and swirled and danced and glided.

Topaz sent ray after ray after ray high into the sky. Diamond blew them into a spin, forming a giant *O* above Gemstone Valley. Streams of light came off the *O* and settled over each of the creatures below. Everyone gasped, reaching up to touch the light. But before they could, Diamond whisked the lights back up again into a giant spinning globe. They were individuals, but they were also all one, together, just as Opal had shown.

Watching from below, surrounded by all her friends, Opal couldn't have been happier.

SOME FACTS ABOUT OPALS!

COLOR: Opals are usually milky white with streaks of colors that flash like rainbows. The colors are created by light bouncing off tiny cracks and cavities inside the stone.

BIRTHSTONE: Opal is the birthstone of people born in October.

MEANING: Throughout history, opals have been believed to be good luck. They were also considered to symbolize loyalty, hope, and happiness.

FUN FACT: Opals were once thought of as the "stone of kings" because kings prized them as wonderful gifts!

JOIN THE GEMSTONE DRAGONS IN ANOTHER EXCITING ADVENTURE!

Turn the page for a sneak peek . . .

A hint of a storm swirled around Gemstone Valley, but no one minded because the sun was peeking through the clouds and every magical creature was in the fields watching the Gemstone Dragons do tricks with their special powers.

Unifoals, young goblins, and gnome tykes oohed and aahed as Topaz spun in the air until her light power looked like a giant pulsing star. Opal used her power of invisibility to play a game of Now You See Me, Now You Don't. Aquamarine lifted chunks of water out of the river so Pearl could power it into ice sculptures.

Everyone cheered and laughed.

Everyone was having fun.

Everyone except Ruby.

"I'll never be able to use my power right! I'm useless," Ruby cried, as another one of her fireballs sizzled out. "I'm the most useless Gemstone Dragon that's ever lived."

"Oh Ruby," said Opal, her rainbow-streaked scales shimmering as she became visible. "You're not useless at all. You're a wonderful Gemstone Dragon."

"But I never get anything right!" Ruby hung her head.

"That's not true. You do lots of things well." Opal gave Ruby a big smile, but it didn't make Ruby feel any better.

Topaz stopped spinning and landed next to them. "Wha . . . wha . . ." She was out of breath from spinning so fast in the air. "What were you trying to do?"

"Just a trick, like you and the other dragons, but my fire keeps going all over the place."

"I'm sure it's not that bad," Topaz said. "Go on. Show us."

Ruby sighed but said, "Okay."

She took a deep breath. Then the gemstone on her chest began to glow as she blew out a ball of fire. It was small and manageable, but Ruby started to imagine all the bad things that could go wrong.

What if it grew really big and she couldn't control it? What if it lit the grass on fire? What if it fell on Topaz and Opal?

As she was thinking these things, her fireball grew bigger and bigger and bigger. Topaz and Opal had been about to clap their paws at Ruby's power, but the fireball wobbled in the air. Ruby gave a little cry, scared that all the bad things she had imagined would come true. She quickly breathed all the fire back in, then shook her head.

"See? I can't make it work."

"You'll get it," Topaz said. "Don't wo—"

"You have to concentrate more, Ruby," Diamond shouted from where he was using his wind power to lift the unifoals into the air as they giggled. "Here, watch me."

Diamond scrunched up his face in concentration and breathed out a small fireball. Then the diamond in his chest began to glow as he made the wind push the flames so they twisted into the sky. The Gemstone Valley children applauded loudly.

Diamond grinned and bowed down low to his audience.

Ruby's cheeks felt hot and she glared at the ground so no one would see. Diamond had just done a trick with fire and he only had the small amount of fire breath that all the Gemstone Dragons had. Ruby had much more fire power because of her gemstone, but she couldn't control it enough to even bounce a fireball.

"Come on," Diamond said, turning back to Ruby. "Now you try. Concentrate hard."

SAMANTHA M. CLARK is a storyteller, a daydreamer, and the author of a number of books for young readers. Most of the time, she lives in her head with a magical tree, a forest of talking animals, and a sky filled with pink fluffy clouds. Like the Gemstone Dragons, she knows the best power in the world is friendship.

JANELLE ANDERSON is an illustrator who is happiest when bringing the images in her head to life. Some of her favorite things to draw are colorful mountains, sparkly waterfalls, and magical creatures just like the Gemstone Dragons. She loves the outdoors and making people smile, and believes there is a little bit of magic in everyone.